CAN DAVE BE REPLACED?

Dave grabbed the ball. He was desperate to score. But Jo blocked his path. As he drove to the hoop, her quick hands stripped the ball away.

Will had seen enough. "Dave, she's *good*," he said. Dave's face fell. "Not as good as you, obviously," Will quickly added. "Hey, I'm not sure a girl playing for us is a great idea, either, but you've got to admit, she's got the moves. . . ."

"Not so fast," Dave said. He was still too stunned to accept what had just happened. "We're not going to take some girl onto our team because she cans a few lucky shots!"

"Listen, how's this for a deal?" Jo asked. "We'll go one-on-one." She nodded in Dave's direction. "You and me, Blondie. You win, and I'm vapor, I'll disappear. But if I win . . ." She paused, looking at all the Bulls and smiling for the very first time. "I'm your teammate, guys. I'm your brand-new point guard!"

IN YOUR FACE!

by
Hank Herman

BANTAM BOOKS
NEW YORK · TORONTO · LONDON · SYDNEY · AUCKLAND

RL 2.6, 007-010

IN YOUR FACE!

A Bantam Book / February 1996

Produced by Daniel Weiss Associates, Inc.
33 West 17th Street
New York, NY 10011

Cover art by Jeff Mangiat

ISBN: 0-553-48274-2
Published simultaneously in the United States and Canada

Bantam Books are published by Bantam Books, a division of Bantam
Doubleday Dell Publishing Group, Inc. Its trademark, consisting of the
words "Bantam Books" and the portrayal of a rooster, is Registered in U.S.
Patent and Trademark Office and in other countries. Marca Registrada.
Bantam Books, 1540 Broadway, New York, New York 10036.

PRINTED IN THE UNITED STATES OF AMERICA

OPM   0 9 8 7 6 5 4 3 2 1

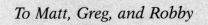

To Matt, Greg, and Robby

IN YOUR
FACE!

CHAPTER 1

The Branford Bulls were sailing in for a classic fast break. Brian Simmons streaked up the right side, with Derek Roberts on the left. David Danzig was pushing the ball up the middle. Dave knew the Bulls had the advantage, since the Essex Eagles had only two men back on defense.

Suddenly Dave's black high tops squeaked to a stop at the foul line. He looked left, then dished to Brian, who floated in for the layup.

1

Bulls 34, Eagles 26! A hush fell over the crowd in the Essex gym. There were only two minutes left in the third quarter.

But as Dave raced back on D, he saw Brian grabbing his right thigh in pain. *Oh, no!* Dave thought. *Bri's got cramps again. Just when we were ready to put the Eagles away for good!*

As Brian clutched his leg and grimaced, Dave looked over at the bench. Jim Hopwood, one of the Bulls' two teenage coaches, put his hands together in a T. Dave knew that meant he should call time-out. But before he could get the referee's attention, Sky Jones, the Eagles' smooth forward, blew by Brian for an easy two points.

Man, thought Dave, *give Sky an inch and he burns you every time!*

Dave signaled for time-out, and the team huddled around Jim and their other coach, Nate Bowman.

"This kills," Brian said. He massaged his leg. "I'm gonna need to sit for a few."

Dave pushed his long hair out of his eyes. "Come on, Brian!" he blurted. "Can't you tough it out? You know what happens every time you sit."

This was the third time that day that Brian's leg had cramped up. Branford should be *destroying* Essex. But each time Brian had to rest, the Eagles cut the Bulls' lead down to a hoop or two.

"If I could play, I would," Brian said, annoyed.

"Give him a break, Dave," said Will Hopwood, the team's center and Jim's younger brother. "We'll just do the best we can."

"Hey, you know what I mean, man," Dave told Brian. "Sorry."

Dave heard a sigh and turned to see Nate running his hand over his short flattop as he looked over the team, considering his options.

Brian played forward and had a deadly fadeaway jumper. Because of that classic move, and his fade haircut, he'd been given the nickname Fadeaway. Dave, at point guard, handled the ball as if he'd been born with it attached to his arm. Will was the Bulls' center and most complete player. His tough rebounding and leadership gave the Bulls their edge.

The three boys had been best friends since kindergarten. Every day they played b-ball on the Jefferson Park playground courts, since their small town, Branford, didn't have a community center. Will, Brian, and Dave formed a solid core that had kept the Branford Bulls together as a team even after two of their founding members and the original coach had moved away a few weeks before. Luckily, Will's older brother, Jim, and his best friend, Nate, co-captains of their high-school team, had agreed to step in and coach the Bulls.

The Bulls' other forward was Derek Roberts. He was a quiet, tall, razor-thin kid with lightning-quick moves. Mark Fisher, the starting shooting guard, was short, with brown hair. Even though he wore goggles like Horace Grant's, he had no problem finding the net from downtown.

There was no doubt the starting five were as good as any team of ten- and eleven-year-olds in the Danville County Basketball League. But with Brian out, the Bulls were down to only one choice.

"Put me in, Coach. Chunky is ready to do his thing!" Chunky Schwartz was as easygoing as he was big. Sitting down, he was almost as tall as Mark was standing up. And no matter how many days the team practiced in the hot summer sun, he always stayed pale. Not even a freckle.

"Okay," Nate said, pointing at Chunky. "You're in for Fadeaway. Be tough on the offensive boards. Let Dave bring the ball up. All of you guys do your best to help Chunky with number thirty-seven. You gotta shut him down!"

Dave knew Nate was talking about

Sky Jones. Even though Brian had been in Sky's face the whole game, he still had scored most of the Eagles' points.

"All right, hands in," Will said. "On three. One, two, three—"

"Bulls!" they yelled.

The crowd clapped and chanted as the teams headed back out onto the court. Even though the stands were full of Eagles fans, the sound of all that cheering still thrilled Dave.

Will inbounded the ball to Dave. Dave kept it low as he moved up the court. He reached the three-point line, dribbled behind his back, and suddenly whipped a sharp no-look pass to Chunky in the right corner. Chunky grabbed it and rushed a pass to Will in the paint. The ball bounced off Will's foot, right into the hands of the Eagles' speedy point guard.

"Nice pass, you big klutz!" shouted a voice from the stands. Dave didn't need to turn around to know who it was. *Oh, man, now Otto and his loser tagalongs are here! How many times do we have to crush the Slashers on the court before they get off our backs?*

The Bulls' rivalry with the Sampton Slashers went back a long way. The Slashers were the only really tough match the Bulls had, but they were a really sleazy team! And Otto Meyerson was the sleaziest of them all. He loved to cheat, and his trash talk was legendary. He was the last person Dave needed in the stands right then.

Dave tried to concentrate on the game. The Bulls were hustling back on defense. The Eagles cleared out the right side so Sky could work one-on-one against Chunky. Sky threw a few ball fakes to knock Chunky off balance. Then he pump-faked to make Chunky leave his feet. As Chunky came down, Sky drove around him to lay one in off the glass.

Ouch! Chunky got schooled! thought Dave.

Dave brought the ball upcourt. Super-fast, he crossed the ball between his legs, then tried to spin past three Essex defenders. But he couldn't do it all by himself. The Eagles' wide-bodied small forward stripped him and pitched an outlet pass to their point guard, who was flying to the hoop.

To Dave's relief, the guard blew the layup, and Chunky muscled in for the rebound.

"Way to go, Chunky!" Brian yelled from the bench.

But then Chunky began to ramble up the court with the ball. Mark and Dave's screams came too late: Chunky's awkward, high dribble made him an easy target for a steal. Another Bulls turnover!

"That's all right, Chunky!" Brian yelled. "Keep at 'em!"

Chunky's face turned bright red as he lumbered back.

The Eagles got the ball to Sky. But

this time Derek and Will rushed in with Chunky to triple-team him. Three sets of arms waved like windmills, yet Sky somehow managed to find one of the Eagles' guards with a bounce pass.

And with Will busy helping out on Sky, the Eagles' big-boned power forward was open. He caught a quick pass and popped the ball in for two.

The Bulls' lead was down to 34–30! The crowd rose to their feet, stomping and cheering the home team's comeback.

"Nice D, Hopwood, you goon! My *grandmother* could smoke you!" It was Otto again from the stands.

Dave started to turn around but changed his mind. *That's just what the Slashers want.* If Will could let it slide, so could he.

The clock was running out. Dave pounded the ball up the floor to get in a last shot. He blew past half-court, pulled up at the three-point line, and let fly, but his shot was way off the mark.

Buuuzzz!

Just like that, the third quarter was over. Dave had to admit things weren't looking good. If the Bulls didn't get it back together pronto, their lead would be history.

There was only a minute and a half left in the game. Jim and Nate had switched the team to a box-and-one defense. Derek was shadowing Sky wherever he went. Will and Chunky played the blocks, and Dave and Mark patrolled the foul line.

They had managed to shut down Sky, but Branford had fallen behind by a bucket. The score was 44–42. From his position on the court, Dave could see Brian getting ready to check back in. The Bull's forward tested his leg, then walked with a slight hobble to the scorers table.

At the next whistle, Brian hustled out onto the court, pointing at Chunky.

"Nice work, dude," Brian said. He slapped five with Chunky as they passed each other.

Chunky was out of breath and looked relieved. "Go get 'em, Brian," he huffed.

Dave smiled, happy to see Brian back on the court, and Will rushed up to Brian with the Bulls' trademark low five.

"Show time!" they said together.

On their next possession, the Bulls picked up the tempo. They moved the ball smoothly around the outside, then Derek whipped it to Will in the pivot. He turned and leapt for the jumper, but—*Smack!* The ball was slapped out of his hands.

The Eagles launched the ball to Sky Jones as he raced up the court. He caught the ball on the run and put up the shot. But at the last second Brian got a hand in front of his face. Sky's shot clanged loudly off the back iron. Not even close!

"Mine!" Derek shouted, crashing the boards. Now it was the Bulls' ball with just twenty-two seconds left. Derek handed the ball off to Dave. Dave shot Brian a look, and Brian nodded back.

Dave brought the ball across mid-court. At the three-point line, he dished the ball to Brian. Derek set a solid pick to the left of the key along the base-line—Brian's sweet spot. Brian dribbled around the pick, ran his man into Derek, and calmly canned the open ten-foot jumper. *Yes!* Dave thought.

Tie score!

"Full-court press!" Will called.

The Bulls swarmed the Eagles as

they tried to inbound the ball. But the Eagles snuck the ball cleanly to their awkward small forward. To Dave, it looked as though the last thing the forward wanted was the ball at crunch time!

Will bore down on him fast, trapping him near the baseline. The kid crouched low and dribbled once. Desperately he twisted, leapt, shot *at the wrong basket*—and scored! Two points . . . for the Bulls!

Buuuzzz!

The game was over. The Bulls had won. Chunky rushed out onto the floor. "We did it!" he howled. "Amazing ending! But of course I always knew we'd win," he added.

The Bulls gathered around their coaches and chanted, "Two, four, six, eight, who do we appreciate? Eagles! Eagles! Yeah, Eagles!"

The teams shook hands and walked toward the locker rooms. Dave looked at Will. "We lucked out this time," he said.

"We're gonna need more than luck when we play a *real* team," Will said, wiping the sweat off his forehead. "We should've blown these guys away."

Dave knew Will was right. The Bulls needed some serious beefing-up of their bench—or they could forget about winning the championship.

CHAPTER 2

Dave's jumper from the right of the foul line fell with a thud to the black-top. Not even close! And that shot was usually automatic for him.

"NBA," Mark kidded good-naturedly, peering at Dave through his goggles. "Nothing but air! What's up, Droopy? Pressure too much for you?" Dave's nickname was Droopy because he wore the baggiest shorts in the neighbor-hood, and because his long blond hair was always falling over his eyes.

They were playing Horse, and Dave and Mark were the only two Bulls left in the game. Mark backed up way beyond the three-point circle and let loose his awkward-looking one-handed heave. As usual, it was right on target.

"Sorry, Dave. Tough act to follow, huh?"

Dave didn't even bother going after the ball. He just let it roll onto the grass. "That's *H-O-R-S-E* for me," he said without expression. "You win."

But it wasn't the game of Horse that had Dave down. It was the close call against the Essex Eagles—who weren't even that good a team. Dave felt as if the Bulls had lost by forty points rather than won by two.

"I guess that's it for today," Dave said, sprawling on the ground with his teammates. It had been a hot, sweaty day. The blacktop in Jefferson Park was actually getting gooey as the heat softened the tar. The Bulls had to sit on the grass alongside the court so their shorts wouldn't stick to the steaming surface.

Mark, the team clown, tried to snap Dave out of his dark mood. "Cheer up, Dr. Doom," he said to Dave. "At least you can *see*." Mark was busy with his familiar routine of using the bottom of his shorts to try to clear up his prescription sports goggles. They always fogged up on hot days.

"Besides," Mark continued, "in case it slipped your poor overworked brain, it so happens we actually *won* on Saturday."

"Yeah, we won," Dave admitted, "but only because that big goof from Essex messed up in the clutch. I don't know about you guys, but *I* wouldn't put that one in the Bulls' highlight video."

"Let's look on the bright side," Will said. "You burned their guard all game. I stuffed that big guard a *minimum* of five times. And at least Brian made Sky work for his points. Okay, so maybe we were a little off here and there. . . ."

"A *little* off?" Dave echoed. "We blew ten-point leads every time Brian had to sit out!"

Dave saw Chunky's face go red, and regretted what he had just said.

"I know I didn't exactly shut down Sky when I was in there—" Chunky began.

"Hey, man," Brian jumped in, coming to Chunky's defense, "Sky Jones would make *anyone* look bad. That dude can *play*."

"Brian's right," Dave said. "All I'm saying is, it's gonna take eight or nine strong guys to finish on top in this league. And we're not quite there yet."

"Dave, chill out," Will said. "We would have shredded the Eagles if Brian's leg hadn't cramped up."

"But that's just the point, Will," Dave replied. "His leg *did* cramp up. Things like that happen. We can't always win with just our starting five."

"If you want to worry, go right ahead." Will grabbed the ball and started spinning it on his finger. "All I know is, we're two and oh. We can't be *that* bad off. You sure something else isn't eating you?" he asked.

There was, but Dave wasn't sure if he wanted to get into it.

"Okay," he said finally, "you guys really wanna know what's got me ticked? It's Otto Meyerson and his loudmouthed buddies. Those guys from Sampton were dissin' us big-time. Meyerson said we're the only team that could make the L.A. Clippers look good! Man, I just want to beat them so *bad*!"

"I'm with you," Brian agreed, nodding. "I heard Otto yapping the whole time during the Essex game."

"If we don't beat those guys," Dave continued, "our whole season will be a bust. We need an extra spark, a secret weapon. Who do we have coming off the bench to give us that kind of lift?"

Dave could tell Chunky wanted someone to mention his name, but nobody did. Chunky was good enough to be a Bull, but not good enough to make a big difference at crunch time. Dave felt bad, but he wasn't going to lie to Chunky. That wouldn't help the problem at all.

A surprise voice was heard. It was Derek, who usually kept his thoughts to himself and let his playing do the talking.

"Any of you guys hear about a kid called Joe? They say he can shoot the ball better than Sky Jones and dribble better than Da—"

Derek caught himself before finishing the thought. Dave could tell that Derek didn't feel like getting into a big debate with him over who was the best ball handler around.

"Anyway," Derek continued, "he might be worth a look."

Dave's interest had perked up. "Joe who?" he asked.

"Got me." Derek shrugged. "They just call him Joe. I think he's from Sampton, but for some reason he doesn't want to play on their team."

"I can't imagine why," Mark said sarcastically. "You couldn't *pay* me to play for Sampton. But I've heard about this guy, too. They talk about him around the playgrounds like he's

20

the next Michael Jordan or something."

For the first time all day the cloud lifted from Dave's spirits. He picked up the ball and easily sank a beautiful fifteen-foot jumper. This time,

NOTHING BUT NET.

A seventh man, he thought. *Instant offense off the bench. No way the Slashers could touch us if we had that!*

"Hey, Mark," Dave said, casually dribbling between his legs. He was trying not to sound as excited as he really was. "Think maybe you could find this Joe and get him to come around to Jefferson?"

Mark had finally gotten his goggles gleaming to perfection, the way he liked them. He put them back on and smiled at Dave.

"I'll give it a shot, Droopy," Mark said.

CHAPTER 3

On Thursday afternoon Dave and Brian were finishing off a tough game of Knockout when something caught their eye. There was a kid approaching along the narrow, paved path that led to their court. Dave knew everyone who hung out at Jefferson, but he had never seen this kid before.

The newcomer wore long, baggy shorts and white hightops with no socks. He also wore a green baseball cap that Dave figured was meant to keep his brown hair from flopping into his eyes. If that's what the cap was for, though, it wasn't working.

But it wasn't what he looked like that made Dave and the rest of the Bulls stop their game and stare. It was what he was doing with a basketball.

"Look at that!" Brian said in amazement. "Between his legs, behind his back. Without even *thinking*! Hey, Dave, is this the guy who taught you your moves?"

"In your dreams," Dave replied. But he had to admit the guy was smooth.

When the new kid got to the edge of the blacktop, he spun the ball easily on his right index finger for about twenty seconds. He snapped his gum loudly. Finally, in the most sarcastic tone imaginable, he said, "Excuse me, but would this be, by any chance, the home of the world-famous Branford Bulls?"

It wasn't until they saw the kid close up, and heard the voice, that they realized the incredible truth: *he* was a *she*.

Dave shot an accusing look at Mark. Mark smiled his goofy smile. "Hey," Mark said, "you asked me to find Joe and bring him to Jefferson. Well," he said, pointing at the girl, "here she is."

The girl seemed to get a kick out of the confusion. "My name's Jo," she announced, "with no *e*. My friends call me Dime."

Dave found himself getting annoyed. He wasn't sure why. "My name's David, with two *d*'s," he snapped back, looking around at the other Bulls for approval. Then curiosity got the best of him. "Why Dime?"

"Because Anfernee Hardaway is called Penny—and I'm ten times as good."

A few of the Bulls laughed at her reply, but Dave didn't find it funny. *This girl needs a serious attitude adjustment,* he thought.

"Listen, *Dime,* you have a last name, too?" he asked.

"Meyerson."

"Meyerson?" repeated Dave. "As in *Otto* Meyerson? That jerk on the Slashers?"

"Yeah," Jo confirmed with a knowing smile. "Otto's my older brother. I'm ten, he just turned eleven. And you're right. He's a world-class jerk. He's stolen all my best moves."

"Listen, Nickel, or whatever you call yourself," Dave said. "I hate to hurt your feelings or anything, but if you're such a pro, why don't you just go play for the Slashers with your brother?"

Jo looked at the ground. "They don't let girls play on their team."

"Well, how 'bout that?" Dave said. "For the first time in my life, I *agree* with the Sampton Slashers! Fact of the matter is, we don't let girls play on *our* team, either."

"Oh yeah?" Jo replied, her face turning red with anger. "I saw your *team*, if you want to call it that, almost blow the game against Essex last Saturday. And if Mark hadn't kept bugging me after he saw me playing outside the

Sampton gym, I wouldn't be wasting my time here now. But he said you needed a really good player, so I figured I'd give you guys a break. It seems to me you *need* one."

For once, fast-talking Dave couldn't think of anything to say. This Jo was so sure of herself. She wasn't at all like the other girls he knew.

So far there had been nothing between Dave and Jo but talk. But now something else was happening. Jo held the ball at the top of the key, facing him. Their eyes met. Dave bent his knees, dropping into a defensive position.

Jo dribbled between her legs a few times, like Michael Jordan starting a move. Then, without warning, she drove to her left. Dave, frozen by the lightning-quick move, just watched as she made the easy layup.

"You like being a spectator?" Jo taunted, throwing the ball at his chest.

It was Dave's turn now. He found it hard to take a deep breath. All eyes were watching him.

Dave dribbled in from the top of the key slowly, deliberately, without his usual self-confidence. His knees felt a little shaky. He stopped at the foul line, gave one pump fake, then went up for the shot.

"Get that stuff *outta* here!" Jo yelled as she leapt high in the air and slammed the ball back. It went speeding to the sideline, where Chunky accidentally stopped it with his nose.

How did she do that? Even though the Bulls were silent, Dave could see how impressed they were. He felt hot with anger and embarrassment. He needed to score quickly.

In too much of a hurry, Dave made a wild heave from the right corner and missed. Jo rebounded, and this time Dave was determined to stop her. Jo faked a drive, then squared up for a three. Nothing but net!

Dave grabbed the ball. He was desperate to score. He wanted to go to his right, but Jo blocked his path, forcing him to his left. As he drove to the hoop, her quick hands stripped the ball away.

Jo stood there, casually spinning the ball on her finger, as she had when she first arrived. "Lose something, Righty?" she teased.

Will had seen enough. "Dave, she's *good*," he said. Dave's face fell. "Not as good as you, obviously," Will quickly added. "Hey, I'm not sure a girl playing for us is a great idea, either, but you've got to admit she's got the moves. . . ."

"Not so fast," Dave said. He was still too stunned to accept what had just happened. His mouth was so dry he had trouble talking. "We're not going to take some girl on our team just because she walks onto our court and cans a few lucky shots!"

"Listen, how's this for a deal?" Jo asked. "We'll go one-on-one." She nodded in Dave's direction. "You and me, Blondie. You win, and I'm vapor, I'll disappear. But if I win . . ." She paused, looking at all the Bulls and smiling for the very first time. "I'm your teammate, guys. I'm your brand-new point guard!"

The Bulls glanced around at each other. Nobody spoke. Dave took a deep breath. *He* was their point guard.

"Just name the day," Jo pressed.

Brian finally stepped forward. "I don't know if a girl belongs on this team, and I don't know if we need a new point guard, either. But if you can beat Dave, you're worth a shot. Come on back here tomorrow afternoon. We'll get the rules straight then."

Dave still hadn't said a word. He swallowed hard. Jo retreated down the paved path, dribbling between her legs and behind her back.

When she was out of earshot, Dave finally announced, "I'll kick her butt tomorrow."

He was trying to sound as cocky as usual. He only hoped his teammates couldn't tell that his stomach was doing serious flip-flops.

CHAPTER 4

It was a quarter to four when Dave, dribbling a basketball, approached the blacktop at Jefferson. As usual, the bottoms of his droopy shorts hung down below his knees. As usual, his long blond hair was falling in front of his eyes.

Dave stopped short. He'd thought he'd heard the sound of bouncing basketballs before he actually caught sight of the court, but figured it couldn't be. He'd made a special point of arriving a half hour before practice was supposed to start.

"Aren't you guys a little early?" Dave asked, trying to hide his annoyance.

"*Early?*" Chunky asked. "Are you kidding? We've been on line since this morning, hoping to get tickets for the challenge of the century."

"Yeah," Mark continued, "it's not every day we get to see our very own Magic Johnson take on the next Rebecca Lobo."

Great, Dave thought. This kind of attention was exactly what he wanted to avoid. Secretly he was hoping that Jo wouldn't show. Or that the Bulls would change their tune and decide not to let a girl try out for the team.

And if the challenge game *had* to be played, he was hoping it would be real low-key. No big deal, just a little one-on-one. Above all, he'd wanted to arrive first, to get in a few confidence-building shots.

No such luck.

Dave pushed his hair out of his eyes and felt sweat on his forehead. It was hot, but not *that* hot. *I must be more nervous than I thought,* he figured.

"Whoa, nice shot!"

It was Will's voice. He was admiring a long bomb by Jo. So Jo was there already, too! She was dressed the same as the day before, except she wore a blue cap instead of the green one.

When did Will and Jo get so buddy-buddy? Dave wondered. Wasn't she the sister of the most obnoxious Sampton Slasher? She could even be a spy! Dave quickly dismissed that thought—the Bulls didn't really have any secrets. But was he, Dave, the only one who didn't like the idea of a girl being on the Bulls?

Dave dribbled to the hoop at the other end of the blacktop and began shooting by himself. Layups, jumpers, finger rolls, hook shots—everything seemed to be going in.

"You're hot today," Brian observed.

Dave didn't answer. He kept on shooting and kept on hitting. He had arrived at Jefferson determined not to be embarrassed the way he had been the day before. *If a girl's gonna beat me,* he told himself, *she's gonna have to beat me at my best.*

When he was satisfied that he had the feel of the ball and that his shot was on, he said to Brian, "All right, let's do it." He tried to sound calm and businesslike. But inside he felt his heart thumping.

"Okay!" Brian called out. Jo and the group of Bulls who had been shooting down at the other end of the court came over to listen. "Here's what we're gonna do. The first man—um, *person*— who gets to eleven wins. Loser's out. Anything that hits the rim or the back-board goes back. Okay, Dave?"

Dave just looked at him. That was the way they *always* played one-on-one at Jefferson.

"Okay, Jo?" Brian asked.

"Whatever you say," Jo replied. "I'm just a visitor here . . . for now." She looked directly at Dave.

"Shoot to see who gets the ball first," Brian said.

"Let her have it," Dave said, hoping to sound as though everything was under control.

"You sure?" Jo asked.

"Sure."

Jo bounced the ball to Dave for him to check it. He slapped it back. The game had begun.

Jo dribbled in to the foul line, stopped, and immediately put up a soft one-hander. The ball bounced around on the rim, then fell off to the right. Dave grabbed the rebound.

After bringing the ball back behind the three-point circle, Dave went into his trademark slow-motion dribble. Left hand to right hand to left hand to right hand, back and forth, over and over again. He kept the ball right out in front of him, where it looked as if it could be stolen so easily. . . .

Jo lunged for it and missed. Dave blew by her for an easy layup. Now it would be obvious to all the Bulls that he had pulled himself together for the challenge.

"Nice move!" Jo said. "You forget that one yesterday?"

Dave said nothing.

"One-zero, Dave," Brian announced. Apparently he had decided to take on the role of announcer and scorekeeper.

"Way to play!" Chunky cheered, pumping his fist in the air.

Well, at least one of the Bulls is behind me, Dave thought. *I guess Chunky doesn't want to lose any more of his playing time to Jo!*

Dave checked the ball for Jo, who launched a long one-hander. Dave was surprised. *A hotshot dribbler like Jo, and she hasn't tried to get by me yet? Could the great Jo be nervous?*

Her shot missed, and Dave won the race for the long rebound. Jo's momentum carried her away from the basket, leaving Dave with a clear path to the hoop. He made the shot easily.

"Nice hustle! I guess the *real* Dave showed up today," Chunky cheered.

"Danzig two, Meyerson nothing," Brian called in his best Marv Albert voice.

Jo took the ball out and drove to the left. Dave stepped in front of her so she had to stop dribbling just short of the basket. His hands were up, and he thought he had her trapped. But she ducked under his arms, took one long stride, and spun the ball in with her left hand. Dave couldn't believe she'd gotten the shot off, let alone scored!

"Vicious move!" Will yelled admiringly.

Who's he rooting for, anyway? Dave thought.

"Two to one, the man in the red trunks leads," Brian called.

For the next few minutes Dave and Jo traded baskets. Dave played with more and more confidence. His dazzling ball-handling, absent the day before, was back. He was also hitting his shots and making some good-looking moves.

After the slow start, Jo got into it,

too. Yesterday's lightning moves, which had kept Dave awake the previous night, were just as awesome this time. But her trash-talking was gone. Dave wasn't nervous, and he could tell that Jo needed her full concentration.

Dave led 8–6. Jo had the ball. She let loose a high-arching rainbow jumper.

SWOOSH!

Then, as Dave tried to back her in, Jo reached in and slapped the ball away. She managed to grab it, turn, and hit a ten-footer.

Dave fell to the blacktop in the scramble for the loose ball and badly skinned his right knee.

Seeing the bright red blood, Jo asked, "You all right?"

"Never better," Dave said. "Keep playing."

The score was eight all. Dave knew he needed to put her away *now*.

He started slowly to his right, then

gave a quick head fake to the left. The move gained him the space he needed to drive around Jo for the layup.

Now it was 9–8, and he knew he had her! He'd just shut her down on D and finish her off with a couple of quick hoops. And that would be the end of all the talk about having a girl on the team. It would serve Will and the rest of the Bulls right for even considering it!

But before he knew it, Jo froze him with a darting move just like the one she'd burned him with the day before. Then, after rebounding Dave's miss, she hit a long bomb to go up 10–9. Watching the ball sink through the hoop, Dave felt his stomach drop.

He drove by her and got off a shot—which bounced off the rim into Jo's arms. She ended the game suddenly with a gorgeous floater, switching the ball from her right hand to her left in midleap.

Dave had lost.

Jo walked over to Dave and extended her hand. "Really good game," she said. "I thought I was dead meat at eight-six."

Dave reached out his hand mechanically. He was in a state of shock. One minute earlier he had believed the game was his.

"Well, looks like Jo's good enough to make the Bulls," Will said, slapping Jo's hand in the team's traditional low five. "Now we just have to clear it with our coaches, but I don't think that'll be a problem." The rest of the Bulls crowded around Jo. Dave had never felt so miserable in his life.

From the center of the circle, Jo asked Dave, "How's that knee?"

Why's she being so nice? he wondered. "It tightened up a little at the end," he answered, "but it's not a big deal." He wanted everyone to think it *was* a big deal, but that he wouldn't use it as an excuse.

"Well, I won't bother introducing you to everyone," Will said to Jo. "I'm sure your brother's told you all about us!"

His teammates laughed.

"I wasn't sure about having a girl play on the team," Chunky admitted to Jo, "but anybody who can drill those shots like you is welcome on the Bulls."

"Listen," Will said, "we might as well get right down to business. We play the Clifton Hawks tomorrow. They've got good ball handlers and a strong inside game, but their shooting bites. What we've gotta do is . . ."

Dave heard Will's scouting report, but not a word sank in. While the rest of the Bulls were looking ahead, Dave's mind was stuck on what had just happened. It was the most humiliating day of his life.

I lost to a girl, he kept thinking. *No wonder they're all hanging around her now. Why would they want to spend their time with a total loser like me?* Actually, it was probably just as well that Jo was getting all the attention. Right then Dave didn't think he could even look his teammates in the eye, let alone talk to them.

The rest of the guys might welcome Jo on the team, he thought angrily, *but to me she's still the enemy—and she always will be!*

He gathered up his towel, his water bottle, and his ball. He followed the Bulls off the court, hanging back about ten steps behind the main group. That same thought—*she's still the enemy*—kept coming back.

Nobody humiliates David Danzig and gets away with it, he thought grimly. *This isn't over yet.*

CHAPTER 5

"Let's skip Bowman's tonight," Will said. Bowman's Market was owned by Nate Bowman's father. It was a great place to kick back and relax with a soda after a game or a practice—and listen to Mr. Bowman's endless stories about basketball. "We gotta get over to the twins' birthday party. I'm sure we can get all the sodas we want there."

The Bulls were in high spirits. It was a summer afternoon, they were looking forward to a game against the Clifton Hawks the next day, and now they had their new secret weapon: a ponytailed

43

girl who could shoot like Reggie Miller and dribble like Magic. As Will had predicted, Jim and Nate had no problem with Jo joining the team—as long as she didn't replace any of the current players.

On top of that, Todd and Ali Simmons' eighth-birthday party was that night.

There weren't too many eight-year-olds a gang of fifth graders would want to spend time with, but Brian's younger brother and sister weren't like other little kids. Because they'd been hanging out with Brian's buddies since they were born, they really knew what was up.

Todd and Ali were also the team mascots, screaming their lungs out at every game. The Bulls wouldn't miss their birthday party for anything.

"I'll meet you guys there later," Dave said casually. "I promised my mom I'd get some stuff done first."

Dave waited until all the Bulls had walked off in the direction of the

Simmons house. Then he headed across the street to Bowman's Market.

"Well, if this isn't an unusual sight," Mr. Bowman said, smiling as always. "Droopy without the rest of the Seven Dwarfs!" Mr. Bowman had a nickname for just about every kid in Branford. He'd been the first to give Will the nickname Too-Tall and Brian the name Fadeaway.

The store owner wasn't used to seeing any of the Bulls on their own. When they came in for sodas after practice, it was always as a team. "Nate, look who's here," Mr. Bowman called out to his son.

"Rest of the guys ditch you and head over to the party? Or weren't you invited?" Nate kidded. He was unpacking cartons in the back of the store.

All the Bulls worshiped Nate Bowman. With his close-cropped hair, his gold stud earring, and his awesome variety of slam dunks, you couldn't get much cooler. Plus he was an excellent coach.

Nate could safely tease Dave about the birthday party. Dave lived next door to Brian and had always been the twins' big favorite. There was about as much chance of Dave's not being invited to their party as there was of Nate's missing one of his thunderous dunks.

"Yeah, I guess I'm not as popular as I used to be," Dave kidded back. But he had to force the joke. He wasn't in a kidding mood.

"What's up, Droopy?" Mr. Bowman asked. "There's obviously something on that mind of yours that you don't think is the rest of the Bulls' business."

Mr. Bowman was a slightly over-weight, balding man who had been quite a ballplayer in his own day. He'd raised Nate himself after his wife died. If there were two things he knew as much about as anyone, they were basketball and kids.

Dave ran his finger around the edge of the Coke can Nate had tossed to him. Even though he had just played one-on-one on a hot summer day, he didn't feel like drinking. He had a tight, funny feeling in his stomach. He wanted to talk, but he wasn't sure how to get started.

"I have this friend who's a really good tennis player," he finally began.

"I didn't know we had any tennis stars on the Bulls," Nate said, but Mr. Bowman raised his hand.

"You don't know this guy," Dave continued. "He's not one of the Bulls. Anyway, this kid got challenged to a tennis match by a girl in his school. . . ."

Dave thought he saw Mr. Bowman wink at Nate, but he couldn't be sure.

"Go on, Droopy," Mr. Bowman said.

"Well, the guy pretty much *had* to accept the challenge. I mean, everyone knew this girl was good, and it would have looked pretty lame if he'd tried to duck out. But he was so nervous he could hardly sleep the night before." Dave looked up and saw the questioning look in Mr. Bowman's eye. "At least that's what he told me, anyway."

"I wonder what made him so nervous, Dave. It was just a tennis match."

"Yeah, but Mr. Bowman," Dave explained, "he was playing a *girl*. He was afraid he might lose to a *girl*!"

"I don't know," chimed in Nate, who had finished unpacking and joined Dave at the counter. "There are some pretty good girl ballplayers in *my* school. Couple of 'em could probably make the boys' varsity. Couple of 'em I wouldn't want to go up against even if you paid me."

"Get outta here!" Dave said in disbelief.

"No, I'm serious. Whaddaya think,

guys are the only ones who can play basketball? Or tennis? Get real, man! You ever watch the NCAA women's finals on the tube? Those girls are tough, man. I mean *tough*! You ever watch that Martina what's-her-name or that Steffi Graf play tennis? Whew! I know *I* wouldn't wanna have to return one of their serves. We're talking *power.*"

Dave finally popped open his Coke and put it to his lips. He considered what Mr. Bowman and Nate were saying.

"So, how'd your friend make out in his match?" Mr. Bowman asked.

"He choked," Dave said. "He blew it. He had a lead, but he blew it."

"Hey, man, that happens to all of us stars once in a while. It's a part of sports," Nate said.

Dave took a small sip of Coke. He was having trouble swallowing.

"Why are you so surprised your friend lost?" Mr. Bowman asked, raising his eyebrows. "You said this girl was pretty good."

"She's *incredible!*" Dave cried. Then, catching himself, he added, "I mean, she's all right, I guess."

"So then what's the big problem?" Nate asked. "This guy's bummed out 'cause he lost to this girl?"

"Wouldn't *you* be?" Dave replied.

"I already told you, Droopy. There's one girl up at the high school who'd probably destroy me if I played her. There's no shame in that."

"But what would all your friends say? I mean, what would all the guys in your grade say?"

"Probably somethin' like, 'That Jessica Purcell crushed big bad Nate Bowman. That girl can *play!*'"

"You don't think they'd make fun of you?"

"Not unless *they* could beat her. Which they couldn't, not in their dreams."

Mr. Bowman, who'd been listening while stacking empty cartons, rejoined the conversation. "Droopy, your friend the tennis player . . . how did his friends treat him when he lost to that girl?"

"Oh, they just made a big deal over the girl. Told her how great she was and everything. Actually, they just kind of forgot about him."

"So you're saying they really didn't make fun of your friend at all?"

Dave thought about it. "I guess not. No, they were just going crazy over this girl superstar."

Mr. Bowman placed the last carton on the pile. "Well, then," he said to Dave, "sounds to me like maybe all the guys in your grade *don't* think it's such a big deal for a guy to lose to a girl. Sounds to me like maybe it's just your friend who has a problem with it."

Dave took this all in.

"Yeah, Mr. Bowman," he said finally. "He does. He's got a *big* problem with it."

CHAPTER 6

"These Hawks aren't gonna know what hit 'em," Brian yapped cheerfully as he headed to the end of the drill line.

"Yeah, the Hawks are probably psyched 'cause they heard we just squeaked by Essex," agreed Mark. With a wicked grin, he added, "Little do they know. . . ."

All this fuss over Jo, Dave thought. *Gimme a break!* It was making him sick.

The Bulls were working their three-man weave to perfection. The ball was whipped from player to player without ever touching the floor. All Dave could hear was the sound of squeaking sneakers on the shiny gym floor.

The Bulls finished their weave drill and broke into their final shoot-around. One long rebound escaped all the way down to the Clifton end of the gym. Chunky chased after it.

"Hey, Schwartz," Dave overheard a thin kid known as Skinny Sam say. "How come you guys are letting a *girl* warm up with you? Getting a little desperate?"

"We'll talk about it when the game's over," Chunky replied as he lumbered back to the Bulls' half of the court.

The team gathered around Jim for the pregame huddle.

"Clifton will probably be a little tougher than Essex, but we're gonna go with the same starting five," the coach was saying. "Two reasons. One, I don't want to shake things up too much, since we've been winning. Two, the Hawks'll probably make less of a big deal about having a girl on our team if we slip her in later."

"Yeah," Chunky said. "I guess you guys heard what Skinny Sam said to me when I went down to get that ball?"

"Loud and clear," Mark replied, "and the way I see it, Skinny Sam's got a nice little surprise coming his way. I hope he's the one who's lucky enough to have to guard Jo."

"It would serve him right," Will said. "Okay. Let's get out there and kick some butt. Hands in. On three. One, two, three—"

"Bulls!" they yelled.

The Bulls started off fast. Mark was on target from the opening tip. He nailed one of his long one-handed heaves to begin the game, and added another two points with a high-arching fifteen-foot jump shot a few minutes later. Brian, to the screams of his parents and little brother and sister, made smooth jumpers from both corners. Will and Derek were sweeping the boards and had scored a basket apiece.

But it was no blowout. Dave was surprised to see that Clifton had added
some decent players since last year.
After one quarter, it was Bulls 12,
Hawks 8.

"Jo, go on in for Mark," Jim said.
"Mark, way to play. We'll get you back
in soon."

"Okay," Mark said. "My goggles need
cleaning, anyway. Eat 'em alive, Jo!"

Dave groaned. "What's wrong with
the combo we have on the floor? We're
doing fine!"

"Dave," Jim said, "you do the playing, and I'll do the coaching, okay?"

Dave bit his lip and shuffled out onto
the floor.

The Hawks' power forward, a muscle-bound, ugly kid known as Bulldog, noticed Jo first. He sidled up to her and said, "Excuse me, miss, may I have this dance?"

Jo just gave him a stony stare.

A few more hoots and catcalls from the stands greeted Jo's arrival on the court. "Ooh, be careful!" some wiseguy yelled from the bleachers. "She might break a nail!"

Dave took it all in. *I knew this would happen,* he thought. Skinny Sam, who was guarding him, said, "Hey, Danzig, who's the cheerleader?"

"Don't ask me," Dave muttered. "She sure wasn't my idea."

The ref blew his whistle to start the second quarter. *Okay, here we go,* he thought. *Let's see if she's gonna try to hog the ball.* Dave was comfortable playing with Mark, since it was clear that Dave was the point guard and Mark was the shooting guard. But before he got much of a chance to brood, Jo quickly took the ball from the ref and inbounded it to him.

At least she realizes who's running the team, he thought.

As he crossed the mid-court line, Dave saw Jo open on his left. He was about to pass to her, but something made him stop. Instead, he worked the ball to Will in the pivot. Will scored on his trademark turnaround jumper.

The next time down, Dave saw Jo wave for the ball. He wanted to pass to her, but the thought of how she'd embarrassed him at Jefferson flashed through his mind. So he ignored her and looked for Brian on the right side of the floor. He managed to find Brian with a hard bounce pass, but Brian was being closely guarded and put up a brick.

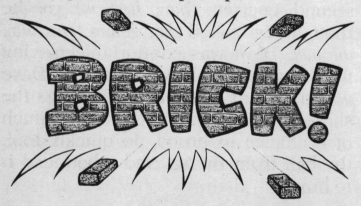

The whole time, the Hawks kept talking trash to Jo. Once, as she ran by the Clifton bench, one of the reserves chanted, "Gimme a *g*. Gimme an *i*. Gimme an *r*. Gimme an *l*. Whaddaya got?"

Jo kept her eyes straight ahead and focused on the game. But Dave looked over at the coaches, exasperated. *If Jo weren't on the team, we wouldn't have to put up with this nonsense!*

Meanwhile, Clifton was staying close. The Bulls held on to the lead, but they couldn't increase the spread to more than four.

Midway through the quarter, the Bulls were running downcourt on offense when Jo shook free from her man and made a sharp cut to the hoop. "Dave!" she called. Dave saw she was wide open and prepared to feed her for the layup. But at the last instant he asked himself, *What am I thinking? I'm not going to pass to a girl!* Instead he forced a cross-court pass to Derek, who was deep in the left corner.

The ball, floating softly, was quickly

snatched by Derek's man. Clifton had a fast-break layup. It was eighteen all.

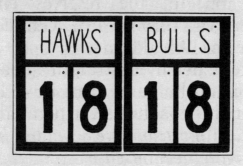

"Time out!" Jim screamed, putting his hands together in a T. Dave could tell he was furious.

"I'm gonna tell you guys a story," Jim said as the Bulls gathered around him. "It's about Michael Jordan's first NBA All-Star game. MJ was the talk of the league, of course, and one of the veterans, who was jealous, thought he'd teach this rookie a lesson. So he froze him out. Never let him see the ball."

Dave could feel the blood rush to his face. He wondered if his teammates noticed he was turning red.

"The player who kept the ball out of Jordan's hands," Jim continued, "is a future Hall-of-Famer—but he'll never live down that selfish freeze-out." He looked straight at Dave. "Now let's get out there and play some *real* ball!"

Dave felt like a kindergartener who'd just been bawled out by his teacher. But the scolding made him more stubborn than ever. The Bulls all hustled back out onto the floor, but Dave waited a moment before getting up from the bench.

"Hey, Droopy, got glue on your shorts?" Nate asked. "I never saw you move so slow. You look like you're going up to get your report card or something."

Dave tried to force a smile but couldn't.

"We wouldn't still be broodin' about our tennis-player friend's problem, would we?" Nate continued.

Dave fired him a look. "You think you know everything. Lay off me, would ya?"

For the rest of the quarter, Dave did pass to Jo, but only when there was no other choice.

On one play he looked for Will in the pivot, and when it was impossible to make the entry pass, he lobbed the ball to Jo on the three-point circle. But the slow pass allowed Jo's defender to get in her face, so she couldn't get off a shot.

A few plays later, Derek signaled to Dave that Jo was open. But Dave's sloppy pass went off Jo's foot and out-of-bounds.

"See what happens when a girl tries to play a man's game?" Skinny Sam hooted.

Skinny Sam and Bulldog had been leading the taunting of Jo since the game began. Now they turned up the volume a notch.

"Illegal ponytail!" Bulldog yelled.

"Careful you don't sweat too much," Skinny Sam chimed in. "It'll ruin your makeup!"

Jo had taken the Hawks' trash-talking and Dave's selfish playing in silence for the entire quarter. Now she glared at Dave.

"I know you think it's a big joke to keep the ball away from me," she said. "Are you also gonna think it's real funny when we wind up losing this game?"

Dave tried to act as if what she said meant nothing to him. "If you don't like the way I run this team, then why don't you quit?"

Dave and Jo were still squabbling as they dropped back on defense. Jo didn't notice a pick set by Bulldog and smacked into him. Dave was too busy arguing to make the switch to Jo's man. The result was an easy layup. Clifton had its first lead of the half, 24–22, with eighteen seconds remaining until halftime.

Dave brought the ball into the front court, but his mind was still stuck on the flare-up with Jo. He wasn't thinking about the time left on the clock. He also didn't notice Derek open under the basket, waving wildly for the ball.

"Wake *up*, Dave!" yelled Jo impatiently as she grabbed the ball from his hands and whipped it to Derek, who flipped it in for an easy two. The Bulls and Hawks were tied as time ran out.

"What the heck were you doing?" Dave screamed at Jo as they headed off the court.

Will answered for Jo. "She was hitting the open man, Dave. That's something *you* might think about doing."

"I've been hitting the open *man*," Dave replied. "I just haven't been hitting the open *girl*." He looked around at his teammates expectantly, waiting for their laughter.

But not one of the Bulls was smiling. To Dave's amazement, they wouldn't even look at him. Maybe they hadn't been incredibly excited to have a girl on the team at first, but Dave saw that all of the Bulls had completely changed their minds—except him. He just stood there as they walked right by on their way to the locker room.

He had never felt so alone in his life.

Dave sat on a bench in the locker room, toweling off.

How could I not have noticed Derek wide open? Man, how totally embarrassing, having the ball stolen by my own teammate! Though he had yelled at Jo about it, he knew she'd done the right thing. And he knew all the other Bulls thought so, too.

Dave looked around. No Jim. No Nate. *Uh-oh,* thought Dave, *one of those team meetings!*

He liked it better when the coaches took charge during halftime, which they usually did. They'd go over what was working and what wasn't, and they'd make the necessary changes.

But once in a while the team would have problems with what the coaches called its "chemistry." Then Nate and Jim would have them meet and try to straighten things out on their own. They had borrowed this idea from NBA teams. Dave thought it was corny.

He noticed one other person missing besides the coaches: Jo. *Aha,* Dave thought. *It's not too hard to figure out what this meeting's gonna be about!*

"Okay, we've got a problem here," Will said. "So let's not mess around. I wanna win this game. I think we all do. But we're gonna win as a team, and Dave's an important part of that team."

Dave made a big show of tying his shoelaces while Will spoke. He couldn't meet the eyes of his teammates.

"It's pretty obvious that Dave doesn't want Jo to be on our team," Will went on. "So maybe we oughta think about playing the second half without her. How does everybody feel about that?"

For a long time there was silence. *Man,* Dave thought, *I wish Jo had never shown up at Jefferson in the first place. Then we wouldn't be in this mess!*

Finally the quietest of all the Bulls spoke up.

"Dave's the man," Derek said, wiping sweat from his forehead with a towel. "But we wanna have our best team out there. And Jo makes us a better team."

Dave tightened up inside. He knew that when Derek said something, it carried a lot of weight.

Will looked at Chunky next.

"Hey, whatever you guys say, goes. I'm just a rookie here," Chunky said. "But I think with Jo in there, we can win big. That give-and-go she worked with Brian early in the second quarter was *sweet!*"

Dave bristled at the compliment to Jo. "Mark could have made that play just as well if he hadn't been picking up splinters on the bench. And speaking of the bench, looks like you won't be seeing a lot of minutes, either, Chunky!"

"I know that ever since I made the team I've complained about my minutes," Chunky said. "Well, last game I got my minutes, and Sky Jones ate me for lunch!"

All the Bulls laughed. Chunky was always poking fun at himself.

"But seriously," he continued, "I can't play D even close to the way Jo did this whole first half. Did you see her stuff that wisecracking dude who called her a cheerleader? She's awesome! I'm not gonna worry about my minutes if she can play like that."

Dave went over to the water cooler for a drink. All of a sudden the locker room felt extremely hot.

Mark, who'd been fiddling with his goggles as usual, piped up. "We're talking about poor Chunky's minutes? *I'm* the one who's probably gonna lose his starting job to that girl!"

Dave felt a glimmer of hope. Maybe he could still get Mark on his side. "That's right," Dave said, trying to egg Mark on. "To a girl who's been to a grand total of *one* practice!"

"You know what?" Mark continued. "I gotta admit I felt a little funny bringing Jo around to Jefferson—though it was worth it to see the looks on your faces. But now? I think she's a *player.* I vote she stays."

The trace of a smile that had briefly appeared on Dave's face disappeared. He didn't have an ally after all. "Yeah, *she* stays," he countered, "and *we* become the laughingstock of the league. You heard Skinny Sam and his buddies today. Well, believe me, it's only gonna get worse!" His voice rose with each sentence. "And what about Otto? How are we going to live down having that Sampton jerk's little sister on our team?"

Finally Brian spoke up. "Dave, I know what you're talking about. I feel a little weird about having a girl on the

71

Bulls, too. And I know we're gonna keep hearing it from the other teams—especially from the Slashers.

"Thing is," Brian went on, "you're a great player. And Jo's a great player. If you two ever started playin' together—I mean *really* playin' together—no one could touch us. Not even Sampton. The Slashers would be history, dude. Imagine it: Otto rocked by his own sister! How sweet would *that* be?"

"Whaddaya say, Dave?" Will asked.

Dave wished he weren't stuck in the locker room with all his teammates. He needed some air. *What they're saying makes sense,* Dave admitted to himself. *If only I hadn't come down so hard against Jo! Now if I back off, I'll look like a total wimp!*

"Look," he said finally, "you guys already know what I think. It was a bad idea for Jo to join the team in the first place, and it's still a bad idea now." His voice trembled, and his hands were shaking. "But you all wanted her, so why don't we stop talking about it?

We're in the middle of a game. Let's go *play*."

Dave took the ball he'd been holding and heaved it against the wall. It barely missed smashing the window. Then he stomped out of the locker room, slamming the door behind him.

"You oughta stick to jump rope! Nobody gets hurt playing jump rope. Or jacks. Now *there's* a game for a girl!"

Dave couldn't believe how obnoxious Skinny Sam was. Skinny Sam had started the game guarding *him*. Now, in the third quarter, he was covering Jo. It seemed he'd made the switch just for the sake of getting in her face.

Man, is this the way I sounded when Jo first showed up at Jefferson? Dave wished he hadn't acted like such a loser.

Trouble was, he'd recognized quicker than anyone how good Jo was, and it made him nervous. *What if she steals my spot as point guard? What if she becomes the one who makes the Bulls go, and they all forget about me?*

But the weird thing was, she didn't seem to *want* to steal his spotlight. He'd never seen such a team player!

Again he cursed himself for making a big deal over trying to keep her off the team. Now he felt he had to stick to his guns.

Dave squirmed as he watched Mark and Jo play the guard positions. He wasn't used to spending so much time on the bench, but he understood why he was out. *Obviously the coaches want what we talked about at halftime to sink in. But I'm not gonna change my tune till I'm good and ready. . . .*

Dave was back on the floor as the fourth quarter began, with the Bulls up 32–30. On the opening play Jo sliced to the hoop,

HAWKS · BULLS ·
30 32

but was fouled hard on the shoulder and knocked to the floor by Skinny Sam.

Dave was the closest Bull to Jo. She looked at him to help her up. *All right, enough is enough. Give her a hand,* he thought. *You'd do it for any of the guys.* But something held him back.

"You're playing with the big boys now," he told her instead. "Take it like a man."

On the next Hawks' possession, Jo hustled into position for a rebound, but Bulldog pounded her on the back while the referee was looking in the other direction. Jo crumpled to the floor again. *How can they keep doing this to her?* Dave wondered. But he didn't do anything to stop it.

Jo was hand-checked or pushed every time she touched the ball, but never obviously enough to alert the ref. Through it all, Dave noticed, her expression never changed. She never lost her tough, calm attitude.

Then it happened.

Jo drove the lane to set up a dish to

Derek. But just before she could pass, she was met by two Hawks and all but tackled. It was clear to Dave that they weren't going for the ball. Their body check had nothing to do with winning the game. It was just sheer meanness.

As Jo untangled herself from the Hawks players, Dave saw blood dripping from her nose. But more than that, he saw that her head was lowered. The fight had finally gone out of her eyes.

It was her downcast look that made him snap.

She's been taking it like a pro all game, and I haven't done a thing to help her, Dave thought. *I don't think I could have hung in there nearly as long.*

In a fury he went flying after Skinny Sam, one of the Hawks who'd taken Jo down. "No one messes with my teammate and gets away with it!" Dave shouted, and shoved Skinny Sam hard in the chest, sending him sliding backward along the smooth gym floor. Then Dave dove on him to continue the attack, but was pulled back by Will and Brian.

"Cool down, Droopy!" Will shouted. "Look, the ref's already hit you with a technical. The last thing we need is for you to get booted out of here right now!"

"Hey, go easy on our hero. He was only trying to come to the rescue of my poor wittle sister."

Dave immediately recognized the obnoxious, sarcastic voice. It belonged to Otto Meyerson. *Doesn't he have anything better to do than follow the Bulls around from gym to gym? The guy oughta get a life!*

Dave struggled out of his teammates' grip. He straightened his baggy shorts and checked his face for damage. Then he went over to see how Jo was doing.

"It's not a big deal," Jo said. "Just a bloody nose."

"Yeah, not a big deal. You look like you're ready for the emergency room. What a bunch of animals!"

"Hey, you weren't so tame yourself! Thanks for helping out. Sorry you got dragged into that mess."

Dave was relieved that she'd said the word *sorry* first. That made it a lot easier for him.

"*You're* sorry?" he blurted out. "*I'm* sorry for acting like such a jerk since you came to join the team. You beat me at Jefferson fair and square."

"Hey, that's history," Jo said. "We're both Bulls now. Who *cares* what happened when we played each other? Now it's what we can do *together* that counts."

The Hawks made the technical, but that was the last point they got.

During the final five minutes, the Bulls played their best ball of the season. Their zone defense was ferocious, cutting off all the Hawks' hopes of penetrating. They picked for each other, setting up one open shot after another. They whipped the ball around the three-point circle so quickly there was no way the Hawks' defense could react.

Most impressive of all was the guard play. Dave and Jo worked together as if they'd been team- 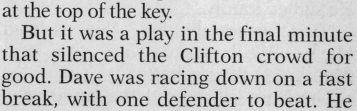 mates for years. On the first play after the fight, Jo drove hard to the hoop, drawing three defenders to her. At the last instant she passed the ball back out to Dave, who was wide open at the top of the key.

But it was a play in the final minute that silenced the Clifton crowd for good. Dave was racing down on a fast break, with one defender to beat. He went up for the shot, and just as he was about to be fouled, he dumped the ball behind him without even looking at Jo, who was trailing on the play. She made the layup easily.

"Poetry in motion," Nate marveled. "It's like watchin' Clyde and the Pearl."

"Like watchin' *who* and *who*?" asked Mark, who was seated on the bench next to Nate.

"Sorry, Mark," Nate said. "I was talkin' about Walt Frazier and Earl Monroe. New York Knicks from *way* before you were born—before my time, too, but you gotta know your history. I'll tell you 'bout them when we've got some time."

"Looks like we'll have lots of time, the way Dave and Jo are playing together. I think I've earned myself a permanent seat on the bench," Mark said. He sighed loudly.

"Don't worry about it," Nate assured Mark. "We'll make sure you and Chunky get your minutes."

The Bulls closed out the game on a

13–0 tear. The final score was Branford 49, Clifton 35.

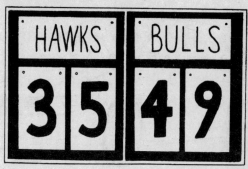

"The winner, and still undefeated!" Chunky roared like a boxing-ring announcer. "The Branford Bulls!"

"Our best game yet, no question," Brian agreed. "We were *awesome!*"

"We want the Slashers! We want the Slashers!" The chant was started by Mark, and the rest of the Bulls picked it up. *"We want the Slashers!"* they roared together on their way out of the gym.

As they headed for the Bowman's Market van (the Bullsmobile, Brian had named it) Will draped his long arms around Dave and Jo. "Whew," he said, "that's two incredible games in a row! Last week's squeaker against

Essex, and now this blowout. I don't know which was more spectacular."

"No contest!" Dave replied. "Last week at Essex, that was just a win." Looking at Jo, he said, "Today was something else. Today was the day we became a *team*."

About the Author

Hank Herman is a writer and newspaper columnist who lives in Connecticut with his wife, Carol, and their three sons, Matt, Greg, and Robby.

His column, The Home Team, appears in the *Westport News*. It's about kids, sports, and life in the suburbs.

Although Mr. Herman was formerly the editor-in-chief of *Health* magazine, he now writes mostly about sports. At one time, he was a tennis teacher, and he has also run the New York City Marathon. He coaches kids' basketball every winter and Little League baseball every spring.

He runs, bicycles, skis, kayaks, and plays tennis and basketball on a regular basis. Mr. Herman admits that he probably spends about as much time playing, coaching, and following sports as he does writing.

Of all sports, basketball is his favorite.

Don't Miss These Other Action-Packed Books:

super HOOPS

#1. CRASHING THE BOARD – Available Now!
The Branford Bulls are the hottest team in town and they are ready to own the championship. But then their coach and his sons, two of the Bull's best players, move away. Do the Bulls still have what it takes to be Champions?

#3. TRASH TALK – Available Now!
Will and Brian both try to run the team while the Branford Bull coach goes off to basektball camp. Pretty soon the teams divided – how can they get back the team spirit and go on to win?

#4. MONSTER JAM – **Available Now!**
Slick Wilson is an awesome new player and a great friend of Brian's. Slick hates Will and has a few nasty tricks up his sleeve at the Monster Jam tournament. Will Brian betray Will just to win?

#5. ONE-ON-ONE – **Available Now!**
A nasty foul leaves Will Hopwood with a sprained wrist, but the *worst* thing to happen is that Chunky Schwartz becomes the new starting center! Can Will teach Chunky the right moves to win them the championship?

#6. SHOW TIME – **Available in June!**
When the team's coach, Mr Bowman, is rushed to the hospital with a heart attack, the Bulls have to pull themselves together to win the championship for their hero!

And don't miss next fall's winning lineup! More Super Hoops books due out in September.